Feeding the lambs

Photography by Bill Thomas

Dear Grandma and Grandpa,

I went to stay

with my friend Sam.

Dear Grandma and Grandpa,
I went to stay
With my friend Sam.

Sam lives on a farm.

Dear Grandma and Grandpa,
I went to stay
with my friend Sam.
Sam lives on a farm.

I saw some mother sheep with baby lambs.

Dear Grandma and Grandpa,
I went to stay
with my friend Sam.
Sam lives on a farm.
I saw some mother sheep
with baby lambs.

Sam has two pet lambs.
They always came running
up to us.

Dear Grandma and Grandpa,
I went to stay
with my friend Sam.
Sam lives on a farm.
I saw some mother sheep
with baby lambs.
Sam has two pet lambs.
They always came running
up to us.

We fed them

with bottles of milk.

Dear Grandma and Grandpa,
I went to stay
With my friend Sam.
Sam lives on a farm.
I saw some mother sheep
with baby lambs.
Sam has two pet lambs.
They always came running
up to us.
We fed them
with bottles of milk.

The lambs wagged their tails very fast.

Dear Grandma and Grandpa,
I went to stay
with my friend Sam.
Sam lives on a farm.
I saw some mother sheep
with baby lambs.
Sam has two pet lambs.
They always came running
up to us.
We fed them
with bottles of milk.
The lambs wagged their tails
very fast.

They drank all of the milk.

They were very hungry.

Dear Grandma and Grandpa,
I went to stay
with my friend Sam.
Sam lives on a farm.
I saw some mother sheep
with baby lambs.
Sam has two pet lambs.
They always came running
up to us.
We fed them
with bottles of milk.
The lambs wagged their tails
very fast.
They drank all of the milk.
They were very hungry.

Dear Grandma and Grandpa,
I went to stay
with my friend Sam.
Sam lives on a farm.
I saw some mother sheep
with baby lambs.
Sam has two pet lambs.
They always came running
up to us.
We fed them
with bottles of milk.
The lambs wagged their tails
very fast.
They drank all of the milk.
They were very hungry.
It was fun feeding the lambs.
I want to go back
to the farm again.
Love from Kate